# Everyone Sleeps

MARCELLUS HALL

Nancy Paulsen Books ◎ An Imprint of Penguin Group (USA) Inc.

CONRAD

NANCY PAULSEN BOOKS • A division of Penguin Young Readers Group. Published by The Penguin Group.
Penguin Group (USA) Inc., 375 Hudson Street, New York, NY 10014, U.S.A.
Penguin Group (Canada), 90 Eglinton Avenue East, Suite 700, Toronto, Ontario M4P 2Y3, Canada
(a division of Pearson Penguin Canada Inc.).
Penguin Books Ltd, 80 Strand, London WC2R 0RL, England.
Penguin Ireland, 25 St. Stephen's Green, Dublin 2, Ireland (a division of Penguin Books Ltd).
Penguin Group (Australia), 707 Collins Street, Melbourne, Victoria 3008, Australia
(a division of Pearson Australia Group Pty Ltd).
Penguin Books India Pvt Ltd, 11 Community Centre, Panchsheel Park, New Delhi–110 017, India.
Penguin Group (NZ), 67 Apollo Drive, Rosedale, Auckland 0632, New Zealand (a division of Pearson New Zealand Ltd).
Penguin Books South Africa, Rosebank Office Park, 181 Jan Smuts Avenue, Parktown North 2193, South Africa.
Penguin China, B7 Jiaming Center, 27 East Third Ring Road North, Chaoyang District, Beijing 100020, China.
Penguin Books Ltd, Registered Offices: 80 Strand, London WC2R 0RL, England.

Design by Annie Ericsson. Text set in P22 Underground.
The illustrations in this book were made with ink, watercolor, and gouache on watercolor paper.
Library of Congress Cataloging-in-Publication Data
Hall, Marcellus. Everyone sleeps / Marcellus Hall. p. cm. Summary: "A wide-awake dog looks for a friend in a
nighttime world full of sleeping animals"—Provided by publisher. [1. Stories in rhyme. 2. Bedtime—Fiction.
3. Sleep—Fiction. 4. Dogs—Fiction. 5. Animals—Fiction.] I. Title.
PZ8.3.H1477Eve 2013 [E]—dc23 2012023258
ISBN 978-0-399-25793-3
1 3 5 7 9 10 8 6 4 2

*E*veryone is getting ready for bed.
"Good night, everyone," they all said.

The mom sleeps.

The dad sleeps.

The baby sleeps.

The cat sleeps.

Even the computer sleeps!

*Everyone Sleeps* . . . everyone except me.
Am I the only one who doesn't sleep?

Squirrels sleep in trees.
Rabbits sleep underground.

Horses sleep standing up.
Snakes sleep lying down.

Ducks sleep swimming in a row.
What about plants? I don't know.

Frogs spend their nights
at the bottoms of lakes . . .

A bear sleeps for months before he wakes.

Brown bats sleep on
the ceiling, upside down.
Giraffes take naps with
their feet on the ground.

A polar bear dozes
on frozen ice floes.
And a fish's eyes never close.
Am I the only one who doesn't sleep?

Shrimp, lobsters, squid,
and whales . . .
all creatures of the deep.
But even creatures
of the deep must sleep.

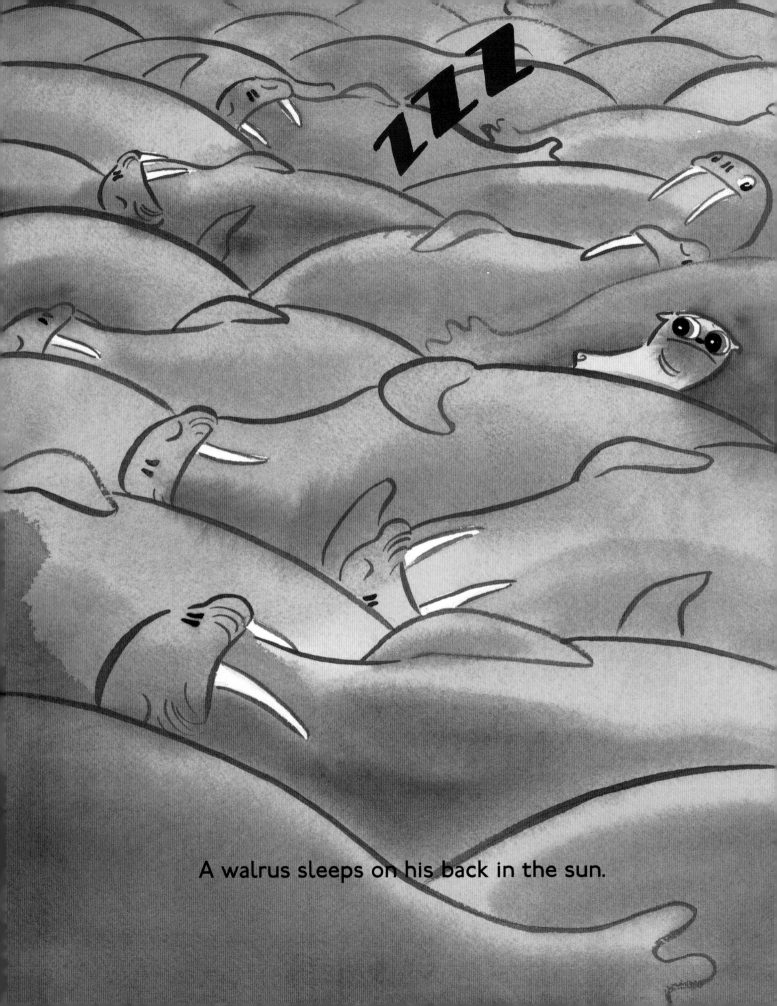

A walrus sleeps on his back in the sun.

This panda and tiger sleep with no one.

Elephants sleep in a herd at night.
A monkey's tail keeps the balance right.

A fox's tail will cushion his head.

And seaweed makes the sea otter's bed.

*Everyone Sleeps,* as far as I can see . . .
everyone except me.

Look at this! It's a herd of sheep . . .
and every one is fast asleep.

How many sheep? A hundred or so?
Maybe a thousand? I don't know.
There are more sheep here than I've ever seen.
I count a few—
*yawn* . . .

then see more in between!

It's lonely when *Everyone Sleeps*

. . . everyone except me.

But wait. Is someone else awake?

Did I make a mistake?

You couldn't sleep, and neither could I.
But maybe together . . . we can try?

*yawn* . . .
Good night, everyone . . .
everyone who sleeps!

Well, almost everyone!